TERRATOPIA

The Graphic Adventure

Special Anniversary Edition
The First Four Tales

Published by

Kids 4 Nature
A division of
THE NATURE COMPANY

TerraTopia

The Graphic Adventure
Special Anniversary Edition
The First Four Tales

The TerraTopia Secret Code Language

A Antenna…
cellular phone for a bug

B Bee…
will sting for food

C Cloud…
as in haze or fluffy white

D Diatom…
snack for a sea snail

E Eagle Print…
hiking boot for a cool bird

F Flower…
a living paint

G Galaxy…
far-out!

H Helix…
spirals in nature

I Icicle…
solid H_2O

J Jellyfish…
hold the P.B.

K Kaleidoscope…
psychedelic

L Leaf…
gatherer of light

M Moon…
heavenly and holey
(you know, like Swiss cheese!)

N Night…
when stars come out

O Owl…
hooter

P Paw Print…
animal's autograph

Q Quick…
as a flash of lightning

R River…
let it flow

S Shooting Star…
meaty meteor

T Turtle…
slow and mellow

U Ursa Major…
the major dipper

V Volcano…
molten blast

W Wave…
water or stadium

X X-ray fish…
Superman of the sea

Y Year…
sublime time

Z Zebra Stripes…
referee of Africa

0 Zero…
zilch, nada

1 One…
as in acorn

2 Two…
eyes

3 Three…
trillium flower petals

4 Four…
wings on a butterfly

5 Five…
points of a maple leaf

6 Six…
sides of a honeycomb

7 Seven…
look at a milkweed seed

8 Eight…
crystal growth

9 Nine…
scorpion bones

293

About 92 billion cans are used each year in the U.S. Lined up, end to end, the cans would wrap around the earth 293 times!

Aluminum Recycling

Billions of cans are produced each year…

… but only 67% are recycled, the rest are left as garbage.

Only 2% of all plastic is recycled. Animals can be harmed if they eat plastic or get tangled in it.

According to legend there are two bears standing in the northern night sky called *Ursa Major* (the great bear) and *Ursa Minor* (the little bear). The Great Bear includes 7 bright stars that make up the Big Dipper. The Little Bear is often called the Little Dipper and it includes Polaris, the North Star. No matter what the season, Polaris is always due north. For millions of years this star has allowed migrating birds to find their way in travels over land and sea.

True North

The earth's axis is an imaginary line that travels from the North Pole to the South Pole. One rotation of the earth around this axis is equal to one day. If you were to follow the axis into the night sky it would point to Polaris or the North Star.

Piper

Something shiny caught Piper's eye as she looked into one of the beach's many tide pools. Thinking it might be a pull tab from an empty soda can, she reached into the water. (Piper always carried an extra bag for trash left by uncaring visitors to the beach.) But to her surprise, the object she pulled from the water looked like a metal dragonfly. Piper liked to collect things so she plopped the key into her pocket.

Bud

Bud pedaled as fast as he could on his bicycle. His grandfather had offered to give him a ride to the gym but Bud figured it was better to use his own energy than the energy required to run Grandpa's old car. When at last Bud arrived in the *Continued on next page*

Weaver ANTS will form a living chain of ant bodies to move supplies or nest members from place to place.

AT LAST THEY REACHED THE TOP. BREATHING DEEP SIGHS OF RELIEF, THE FOUR TURNED TO LOOK AT A SURPRISING VIEW OF THIS MYSTERIOUS PLACE.

There are 3 moons in Terra Topia. One circles this magical land once a year, another once a month and the third once a day. For all 3 moons to be full and appear in the night sky together there is a wait of many, many years.

UNBELIEVABLE!

THE COLORS ARE FANTASTIC!

LOOK—THREE MOONS. WOW!

AND I ALWAYS THOUGHT THE BAYOU WAS COOL...

AS IT BECAME DARK, MAX, PIPER, SKETCH, AND BUD LIT A SMALL FIRE INSIDE THE ROCKY WALLS OF THE WOLF'S MOUTH.

MAX, BUD, PIPER, AND SKETCH SAT IN SHOCKED SILENCE, UNABLE TO MOVE A MUSCLE.

WE ARE THE ELDERS OF THIS ISLAND.

FROM BEHIND THE WOLF, A BEAUTIFUL INDIAN GIRL APPEARED.

WE CERTAINLY HAVE.

YOU SEE, WE'VE BEEN EXPECTING YOU...HAVEN'T WE GRANDDAUGHTER?

MY NAME IS FOXFIRE AND THESE ARE MY GREAT-GREAT-GREAT-GRANDPARENTS—THE KEEPERS OF TERRATOPIA.

COME CLOSER TO THE FIRE AND LET US EXPLAIN WHY THE DOOR TO TERRATOPIA HAS BEEN OPENED TO EACH OF YOU, AND WHY YOUR CLIMB UP TOTEM ROCK WAS NO MISTAKE.

Snakes smell with their tongue and a special gland inside their mouths. They are able to sense molecules of scent in the air and the heat of nearby animals.

BY THE LIGHT OF THE FIRE, A MYSTERIOUS CHANGE BEGAN TO TAKE PLACE. THE SNAKE SLITHERED DOWN FROM THE WOLF, COILING ITSELF INTO A CIRCLE. SLOWLY, THE IMAGE OF AN ANCIENT MAN APPEARED IN THE PATTERN OF THE SNAKE'S SCALES.

WE HAVE BEEN WAITING FOR THE THREE MOONS TO APPEAR, SIGNALING YOUR ARRIVAL.

THE WOLF, TOO, BEGAN TO CHANGE—ITS RICH, WHITE FUR COAT PEELED ITSELF AWAY TO REVEAL A VERY OLD WOMAN.

FOR MANY, MANY YEARS, A SMALL SPIDER HAS BEEN SPINNING A WEB INTO WHICH EACH OF YOUR LIVES HAS BEEN WOVEN. YOUR LIVES ARE NOW CONNECTED WITH THE FUTURE OF THE PLANET EARTH.

FROM EVERY GENERATION, FOUR CHILDREN ARE CALLED TO TERRATOPIA TO LEARN ABOUT SAVING THE EARTH. FROM AMONG ALL CHILDREN IN YOUR GENERATION, YOU HAVE BEEN CHOSEN TO JOIN FOXFIRE IN THE CONTINUING QUEST TO KEEP ALL WILD THINGS FREE AND SAFE.

THE OLD WOMAN OPENED HER HANDS, REVEALING FIVE STONES, EACH DELICATELY CARVED IN THE SHAPE OF AN ANIMAL.

THESE CARVED STONES ARE YOUR PERSONAL TOTEMS. THEY ARE GIFTS FROM THE ELDERS. A TOTEM IS AN ANIMAL CARVED IN STONE THAT HAS MAGICAL POWERS. IT HANGS FROM A CORD AROUND YOUR NECK.
YOUR TOTEM WILL HELP EACH OF YOU IN TIMES OF TROUBLE OR NEED. AND YOUR TOTEMS HAVE MUCH TO TEACH YOU ABOUT NATURE.
MY TOTEM IS THE SNAKE. LIKE THE SNAKE, I AM VERY, VERY OLD. I AM THE LINK TO A TIME WHEN REPTILES RULED THE EARTH. I HAVE LEARNED FROM THE POWER OF NATURE AND ALL LIVING THINGS FOR THOUSANDS OF YEARS. I AM THE SNAKE, OLD AND WISE.
I AM THE WOLF ELDER. I AM THE LEAD WOLF, OFTEN SEEN ALONE IN FRONT OF THE WOLF PACK. LIKE MY TOTEM, I GUIDE MY LOVED ONES THROUGH THE MANY DANGERS AND BEAUTIES OF NATURE. THE WORLD WE LIVE IN IS FILLED WITH MYSTERY AND WONDER. I, THE WOLF, AM NATURE'S TEACHER.
YOUR TOTEMS' POWERS WILL SHOW YOU HOW TO TAKE CARE OF TERRATOPIA AND YOUR OWN PLANET, EARTH. MANY PEOPLE THINK THAT HUMAN BEINGS ARE NOT PART OF NATURE. BUT THIS IS NOT TRUE.
EACH OF US IS CONNECTED TO ONE ANOTHER AND ALL OF NATURE. HUMAN SURVIVAL DEPENDS ON LEARNING MORE ABOUT NATURE AND TAKING CARE OF IT. THAT IS WHY YOU ARE HERE.

FOXFIRE LIFTED THE FOUR TOTEMS FROM THE WOLF ELDER'S HAND AND WALKED OVER TO WHERE MAX WAS STANDING IN FRONT OF THE FIRE.
MAX, YOUR TOTEM IS THE SPIDER. AS SPIDERS WEAVE THEIR WEBS, YOU WEAVE IDEAS TOGETHER TO MAKE PLANS AND SOLVE PROBLEMS. YOU, MAX THE SPIDER, ARE OUR LEADER.
YOUR TOTEM, PIPER, IS THE DOLPHIN. DOLPHINS ARE VERY SMART CREATURES WHO LOVE TO PLAY. YOU HAVE FUN WHILE YOU LEARN. PIPER, AS THE DOLPHIN, YOU ARE EVER PLAYFUL AND KEEP US LAUGHING.
BUD, YOU ARE GOOD AT SPORTS. YOUR TOTEM IS THE MOUNTAIN LION. MOUNTAIN LIONS ARE ANIMALS WITH GREAT POWER. LIKE THEM, YOU ARE COURAGEOUS, STRONG AND FAST. BUD, YOU ARE THE MOUNTAIN LION, WHO GUIDES US THROUGH DANGER.

THE EAGLE IS YOUR TOTEM, SKETCH. EAGLES HAVE VERY GOOD EYESIGHT AS THEY FLY HIGH ABOVE THE EARTH. YOU, TOO, CAN SEE THINGS OTHER PEOPLE CAN'T. YOU CAN SEE WHAT PEOPLE ARE LIKE ON THE INSIDE. YOU SEE INTO THEIR HEARTS. YOU ARE THE EAGLE, SKETCH, WHO HELPS US SEE THE TRUTH ABOUT OURSELVES AND OTHERS.
GRANDDAUGHTER, YOUR TOTEM IS THE FOX. FOXES ARE SWIFT AND VERY CLEVER. THOUGH FOXES ARE SMALL ANIMALS, THEY USE THEIR CLEVERNESS AND SPEED TO OUTSMART BIGGER, MORE DANGEROUS ANIMALS.
FOXFIRE, YOU ARE THE FOX WHO GUIDES THESE CHILDREN ON THEIR ADVENTURES THROUGH TERRATOPIA. SHOW THEM THE POWER AND BEAUTY OF NATURE. HELP THEM LOVE AND CARE FOR THEIR OWN WORLD.

DAWN BEGAN TO SHOW IN THE NIGHT SKY. THE FIRE WAS SLOWLY DYING.
WE MUST GO NOW. OUR TIME IS PAST. YOU CHILDREN ARE THE FUTURE OF YOUR WORLD. LEARN THE MAGIC OF TERRATOPIA TO SAVE THE EARTH.
WHENEVER YOU RETURN HERE TO TOTEM ROCK, WE WILL APPEAR TO YOU AGAIN IN HUMAN FORM. BUT DO NOT FEAR. THE SNAKE AND THE WOLF WILL ALWAYS BE NEAR EACH OF YOU ON YOUR ADVENTURES IN TERRATOPIA.
WHEN YOU NEED THE MAGIC POWER OF YOUR TOTEMS, REMEMBER THE WORDS ON THE MAP OF TERRATOPIA.
THE WOLF ELDER LOWERED HER HEAD AND BECAME THE WOLF ONCE AGAIN. THE SNAKE TOOK HIS PLACE, COILED AROUND THE WOLF'S NECK. TOGETHER THEY STEPPED INTO THE DYING FIRE AND DISAPPEARED.

Triceratops had a large shield of bone to protect its neck, 3 horns, and powerful legs.

Although **Triceratops** was a vegetarian, it may have been a tough dinosaur to push around by larger predators such as Tyrannosaurus.

SOMEHOW I FEEL LIKE I'VE BEEN THROUGH THIS ONCE BEFORE...

SUDDENLY, THE JUN-GLE AROUND THEM BEGAN TO SHAKE AND TREMBLE.

CLEAR OUT, EVERYONE!

Crash!

WHEW! HOW FAST DO YOU THINK THAT BIG LIZARD WAS MOVIN'?

BEATS ME... BUT IT WAS IN SOME KIND OF HURRY.

I DON'T UNDERSTAND... THE ANIMALS HERE ARE GENER-ALLY VERY GENTLE... THAT IS UNLESS THERE'S GRAVE DANGER. AND IF THERE IS...

Eagles have 7,000 feathers covering their body.

&

An eagle's eyesight is 8 times more powerful than your eyesight.

&

With strong claws as feet and a sharp, hooked beak, eagles are able to capture fish and small animals for food. Eagles also eat dead and dying animals.

&

According to Greek mythology, the eagle was the messenger of Zeus because it could grab lightning without being harmed.

Dolphins are social animals that travel in groups called pods. Pod members play, feed, and travel together. Members will care for one another—if one dolphin is sick or wounded, others will push him or her to the surface to breathe.

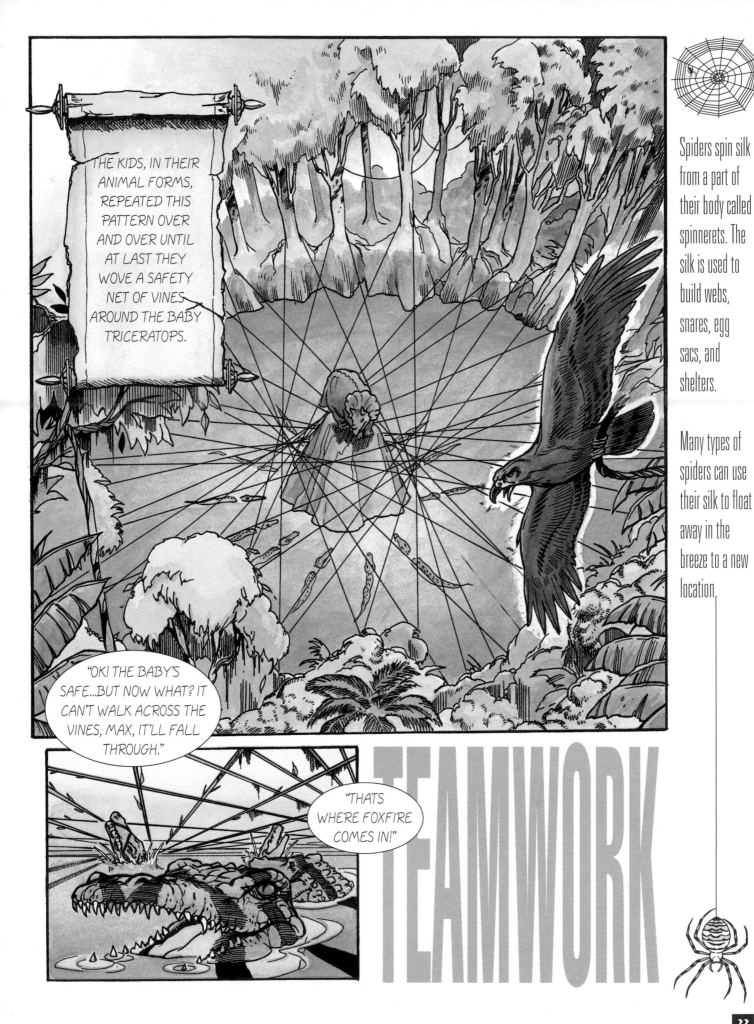

Spiders spin silk from a part of their body called spinnerets. The silk is used to build webs, snares, egg sacs, and shelters.

Many types of spiders can use their silk to float away in the breeze to a new location.

The **Mountain Lion** goes by many as 40 names, including *panther*, *cougar*, and *puma*. Mountain lions walk on their toes, which are called digits. They cannot roar.

AFTER ALL OF THE EXCITEMENT DIED DOWN, FOXFIRE LED THE OTHERS TO A SECRET HIDEOUT IN THE ROOTS OF A VERY OLD TREE NEAR THE BASE OF TOTEM ROCK.
CAN YOU BELIEVE WE RESCUED A REAL DINOSAUR? TEAM-WORK MADE ALL THE DIF-FERENCE—OH, AND THE TOTEMS HELPED.
LET'S GIVE OURSELVES A NAME... HOW ABOUT "TERRATROOPERS"— YOU KNOW ...KIND OF LIKE A TERRATOPIA RESCUE TEAM AND THIS HIDEOUT WILL BE OUR HEADQUARTERS.
EACH OF YOU HAS A SECRET PASSAGEWAY HERE IN OUR HIDEOUT THAT WILL LEAD YOU BACK TO YOUR OWN WORLD. BUT REMEMBER —ALWAYS WEAR YOUR TOTEMS AND CARRY YOUR DRAGONFLY KEY. YOU MAY BE NEEDED IN TERRATOPIA AND YOU MUST USE YOUR DRAGONFLY KEY TO RETURN.
YEAH, WE'LL BE A TEAM AND WE'LL RESCUE THE WORLD!
UH...RIGHT.

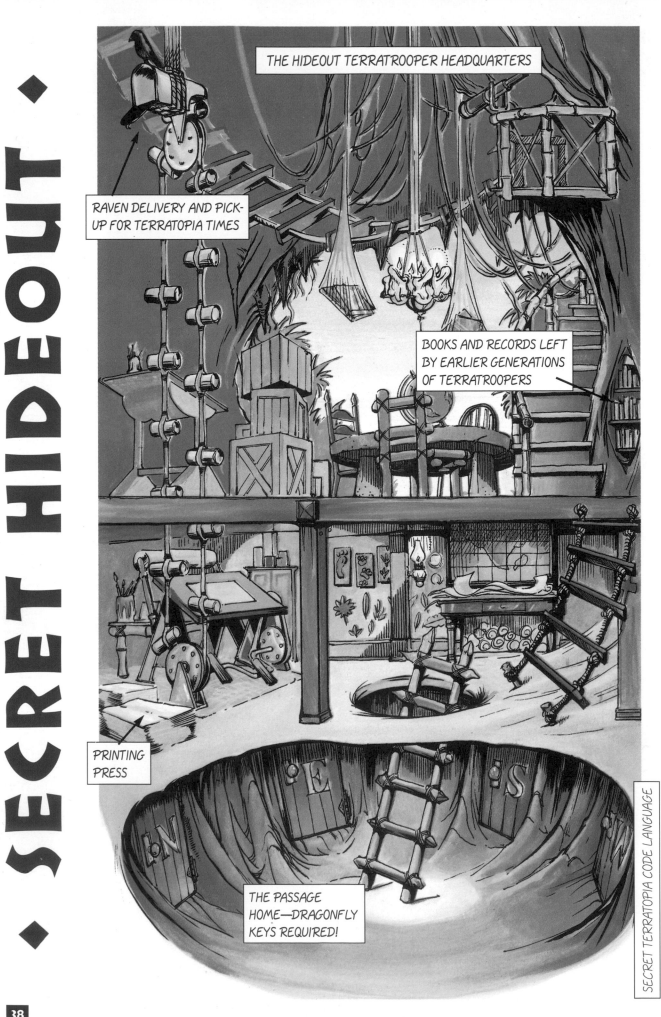

ALL NIGHT LONG, THE WIND HOWLED AND THE WAVES CRASHED AGAINST THE ROCKS. MANY KINDS OF SEA LIFE FROM THE DEPTHS OF THE OCEAN SWIRLED IN VIOLENT WATERS AND WERE TOSSED ONTO THE SOUTHERN CALIFORNIA SHORE.

THE NEXT MORNING, PIPER WOKE UP EARLY AND QUIETLY SLIPPED OUT THE BACK DOOR. SHE COULDN'T WAIT TO EXPLORE THE COVE AND SEE WHAT THE AUTUMN STORM HAD WASHED UP. BUT PIPER WASN'T PREPARED FOR WHAT SHE WOULD FIND.

THAT WAS ONE WHOPPER OF A STORM.

AROUND HER NECK, PIPER WORE THE MAGIC DOLPHIN TOTEM FROM TERRATOPIA. IT WAS A GIFT TO HER FROM THE ANCIENT ELDERS, ALLOWING HER TO MAGICALLY CHANGE INTO A REAL DOLPHIN. IT REMINDED HER OF THE TERRATROOPERS' MISSION TO HELP SAVE THE PLANET EARTH.

SOMETIMES THAT FIRST JOURNEY TO TERRATOPIA SEEMED LIKE A DREAM. RESCUING A BABY TRICERATOPS— WOW! WHEN PIPER WROTE A STORY AT SCHOOL ABOUT HER ADVENTURE IN TERRATOPIA, THE TEACHER DIDN'T BELIEVE HER. BUT THE TEACHER DID WRITE "VERY IMAGINATIVE" ON TOP.

Scallop

Sea Urchin

Periwinkle

Starfish

Hornshell

39

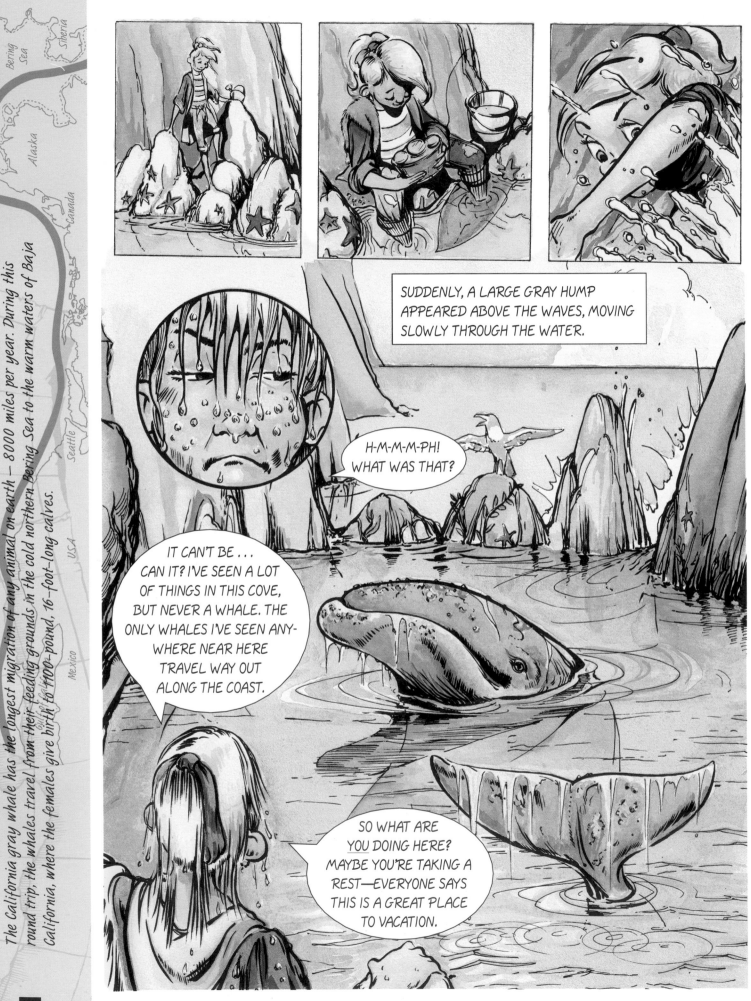

The California gray whale has the longest migration of any animal on earth — 8000 miles per year. During this round trip, the whales travel from their feeding grounds in the cold northern Bering Sea to the warm waters of Baja California, where the females give birth to 1100-pound, 16-foot-long calves.

PIPER COULDN'T WAIT TO TELL HER FRIENDS ABOUT SPOUTER. A REAL WHALE, HERE IN HER COVE! JUST AS SHE WAS DECIDING WHO TO TELL FIRST, SHE HEARD A BUZZING SOUND NEAR HER EAR. PIPER LOOKED AROUND IN TIME TO SEE A DRAGONFLY MAKING ITS SECOND CIRCLE AROUND HER HEAD.

EVERY FEW MINUTES THE DRAGONFLY DARTED TOWARD PIPER, NARROWLY MISSING HER.

MAYBE YOU'RE THE DRAGONFLY FROM TERRATOPIA?

IS THIS WHAT FOXFIRE MEANT BY A CALL FROM TERRATOPIA TO THE TERRATROOPERS? HAVEN'T THEY HEARD OF TELEPHONES?

SPOUTER, I'VE GOT TO GO. I THINK THEY NEED ME IN TERRATOPIA. BUT DON'T WORRY, I'LL BE BACK AS QUICK AS I CAN.

Adult gray whales are 45 to 50 feet in length and weigh up to 30 tons, the weight of 15 elephants!

RELUCTANTLY, PIPER LEFT HER NEW-FOUND FRIEND AND HURRIED BACK HOME.

FROM A SECRET BOX HIDDEN UNDER HER BED, PIPER PULLED OUT THE SILVER DRAGONFLY KEY.

HER QUARTER OF THE MAP OF TERRATOPIA WAS STILL PINNED UP ON THE WALL. PIPER TURNED THE KEY IN THE LOCK ON THE MAP AND STEPPED THROUGH THE DOOR INTO TERRATOPIA.

Sketch:
"I was taking photographs of salmon as they were swimming upstream to spawn."

Max:
"I was sitting on the steps in front of my house, eating a peanut butter, banana and onion sandwich."

Bud:
"I was out for a run in the wetlands."

What were YOU doing when you first saw the dragonfly?

The earth belongs to a huge galaxy of stars called the **Milky Way**. The Milky Way is made up of 100,000 million stars. The earth's sun is only one of these stars. Many different cultures have stories to explain the origin of the Milky Way—Eskimos believe that the Milky Way is the snowy pathway of the Great Raven and Laplanders believe it to be the path of migrating birds. Do you think TerraTopia is in the Milky Way?

Earth is Here

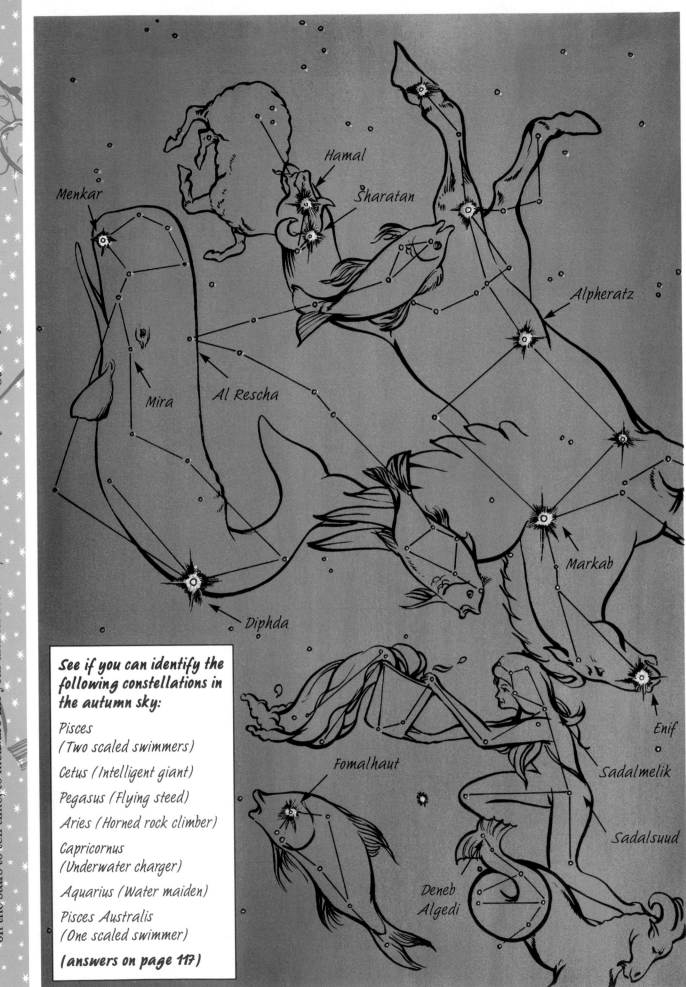

G roups of stars are called **constellations** (*kŏn´ste lā´ shens*). Over thousands of years, different people have seen patterns in the sky and have given those patterns special names. Ancient people relied on the stars to tell time, to measure the year and its seasons, and to find their way on long journeys.

Menkar

Hamal

Sharatan

Alpheratz

Mira

Al Rescha

Markab

Diphda

Enif

Sadalmelik

Fomalhaut

Sadalsuud

Deneb Algedi

See if you can identify the following constellations in the autumn sky:

Pisces
(Two scaled swimmers)

Cetus (Intelligent giant)

Pegasus (Flying steed)

Aries (Horned rock climber)

Capricornus
(Underwater charger)

Aquarius (Water maiden)

Pisces Australis
(One scaled swimmer)

(answers on page 117)

Every community of living things has a **food chain** in which energy is passed from one living thing to another.

IN THE WORLD OF LIVING THINGS, THERE IS SOME-THING CALLED "NATURAL SELECTION" — IT MEANS THAT ANIMALS BEST-SUITED TO THEIR ENVIRONMENT OVER LONG PERIODS OF TIME HAVE THE GREATEST CHANCE FOR SURVIVAL. NATURAL SELECTION KEEPS NATURE IN BALANCE. LIFE IS LIKE A CHAIN IN WHICH ALL LIVING THINGS ARE DEPENDENT ON ONE ANOTHER. DANGER AND SURVIVAL ARE SIMPLY A PART OF LIFE.

SOMETIMES CIRCUMSTANCES DEMAND THAT WE CONFRONT DANGER AND SURVIVAL. THREE DAYS AGO, A SUDDEN FROST BLANKETED THE FOREST IN RAINBOW GLEN. MIGRATING WOLVES SOUGHT SHELTER IN CRYSTAL CAVE. THE ADULT WOLVES REMAINED NEAR THE MOUTH OF THE CAVE, BUT THE WOLF PUPS WANDERED DEEP INTO THE CAVERNS. SOON THEY BECAME LOST IN A MAZE OF ANCIENT LAVA TUBES—TUNNELS THAT ONCE CARRIED HOT MOLTEN LAVA TO THE SEA.

THERE ARE ONLY A HANDFUL OF WOLVES IN ALL OF TERRATOPIA. WHEN DANGER THREATENS, WE MUST HELP THE WOLVES SO THE PACK CAN GROW AND SURVIVE ON ITS OWN.

IN YOUR WORLD, WOLVES ALSO EXIST IN LIMITED NUMBERS AND MUST BE PROTECTED SO THAT THEY DO NOT DISAPPEAR. MANY HUMANS ARE AFRAID OF WOLVES—THEY DO NOT UNDERSTAND THAT WOLVES CAN ALSO BE GENTLE ANIMALS. THE WOLVES IN YOUR WORLD HAVE DIFFICULTY FINDING ENOUGH FOOD AND SPACE TO SURVIVE. NOW PEOPLE MUST INTERFERE WITH NATURAL SELECTION AND PROTECT WOLVES FROM HUMAN AND NATURAL DANGERS IN HOPES THAT THE WOLVES WILL SURVIVE AND NOT BECOME EXTINCT.

Something that is **extinct** (ĭk stĭngkt´) no longer exists in living form. The dinosaur went extinct 65 million years ago, perhaps from a large meteorite landing on the earth. Something that is **endangered** (ĕn dān´ jer ed) is in danger of soon becoming extinct. The reasons are usually due to overhunting or destruction of that plant's or animal's environment.

A volcano is an opening in the crust of a planet through which very hot, melted rock erupts. This fiery rock is called **lava (lä′vä)** once it hits the surface. Mount St. Helens, a volcano in the state of Washington, erupted in 1980 after 123 years of silence. The eruption killed 57 people and destroyed 230 square miles of forest life.

In preparation for winter, many trees lose their leaves. Before the leaves fall, the tree takes in and saves as much useful energy as it can. As the tree absorbs the green portion of the leaf called **chlorophyll**, other colorful pigments such as yellows, oranges, and reds appear.

Ash

Eagle

Deer

Duck

Raccoon

Mouse

Mountain Lion

Hidden Animals

See if you can discover the seven hidden animals: caribou wolf goose dragonfly squirrel monarch butterfly raven

Hint: There are 2 wolves!
(answers on page 117)

Sketch

THE WOLVES GREETED THE TERRATROOPERS AT THE MOUTH OF CRYSTAL CAVE.

LOOK AT THEIR FACES. THEY SEEM SO SAD.

NO JOKE. I SURE WOULD BE SAD IF I LOST MY BABIES.

HOW MANY PUPS DO YOU THINK THERE WERE?

MAYBE WE CAN FIGURE IT OUT FROM THEIR FOOTPRINTS.

LOOKS LIKE THIS MUST BE THE PASSAGE THE PUPS TOOK.

I COUNT FIVE SETS OF PRINTS.

What story do these tracks tell? Who was here? What happened? (answers on page 117)

55

When red-hot lava comes to the surface, it may have a temperature of more than 2000° F. Hawaiians call lava that has cooled into smooth sheets **Pahoehoe** (pah HOH ee HOH ee) and lava that has cooled into rough, jagged sheets **aa** (AH ah).

MEANWHILE, SKETCH HAD CHANGED INTO HIS EAGLE FORM AND WAS SOARING ABOVE TERRATOPIA IN SEARCH OF GAS VENTS.

WOW! IT LOOKS LIKE EVERYONE'S HEADING SOUTH FOR THE WINTER.

Monarch butterflies have extraordinary powers of flight. In the fall they migrate over 2,000 miles from Canada to southern regions where they hibernate for the winter. *Butterfly trees* are the trees where the butterflies rest during their journey. They return to the same trees every year.

PIPER HIKED TO THE COAST BEFORE TURNING INTO A DOLPHIN TO DO HER PART IN THE WOLF SEARCH AND RESCUE OPERATION.

I WONDER WHERE YOU'RE ALL GOING? DO YOU HAVE A HOME OR ARE YOU ALWAYS ON THE MOVE?

DON'T YOU GET TIRED? I SURE AM! WHEN DO YOU GET TO STOP?

Sperm whales feed mostly on giant squid that are hunted at depths of nearly 3,000 feet. The whales can stay underwater for up to an hour at a time.

Orca, or killer, whales are jet-black with distinct snow-white regions. They are able to dive for 4 minutes at a time. The fastest of all marine mammals, the orca can swim 40 miles per hour.

EVERYONE IN TERRATOPIA SEEMS TO BE ON THE MOVE. SOME ARE IN THE SKY, SOME ON LAND, AND NOW I SEE ALL OF YOU SWIMMING... SOMEWHERE.

ACTUALLY, YOU REMIND ME OF A FRIEND BACK HOME... MAYBE SPOUTER WAS TRAVEL-ING TOO. I WONDER IF SPOUTER WANTED TO KEEP GOING AND JUST GOT STUCK IN THE COVE?

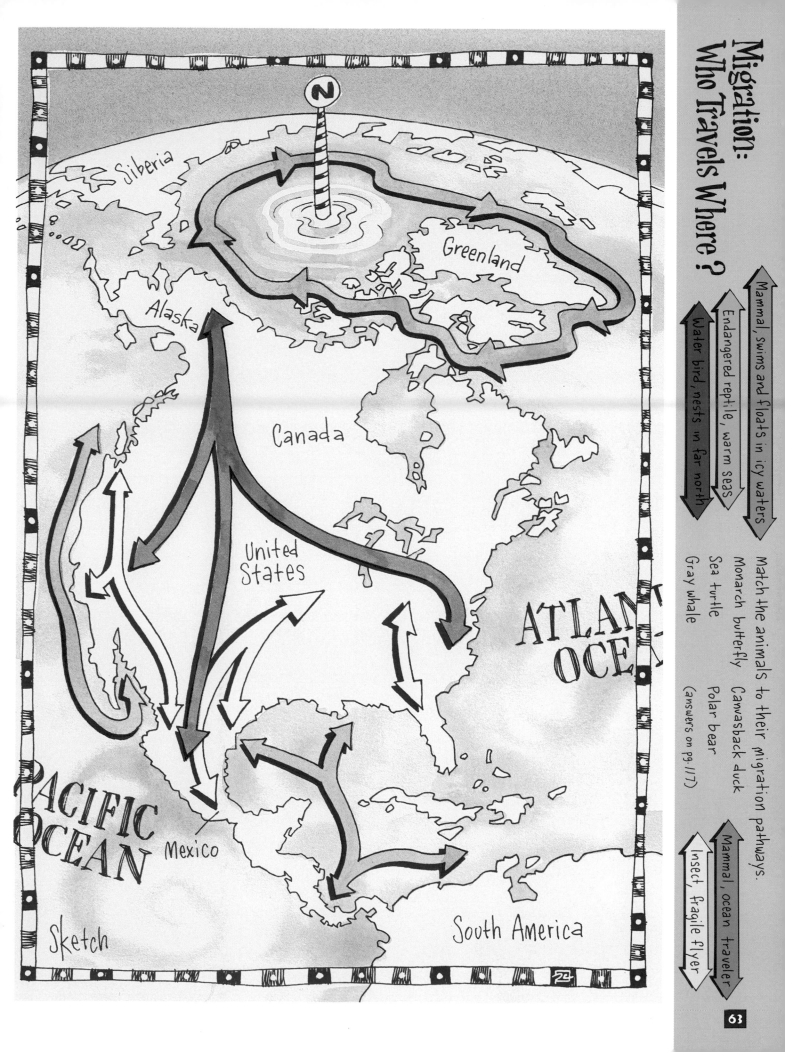

Mammal, swims and floats in icy waters

Endangered reptile, warm seas

Water bird, nests in far north

Match the animals to their migration pathways.

Monarch butterfly   Canvasback duck

Sea turtle   Polar bear

Gray whale

(answers on pg. 117)

Mammal, ocean traveler

Insect, fragile flyer

Siberia

Greenland

Alaska

Canada

United States

ATLAN
OCE

PACIFIC
OCEAN

Mexico

South America

Sketch

63

Dolphins find their way in the water and hunt for food using **echolocation** (*ĕk ō lō kā shen*) or **sonar** (*sō'när'*). By sending out a series of clicking sounds, dolphins are able to listen to the return echoes and determine where something is, as well as its shape and size.

65

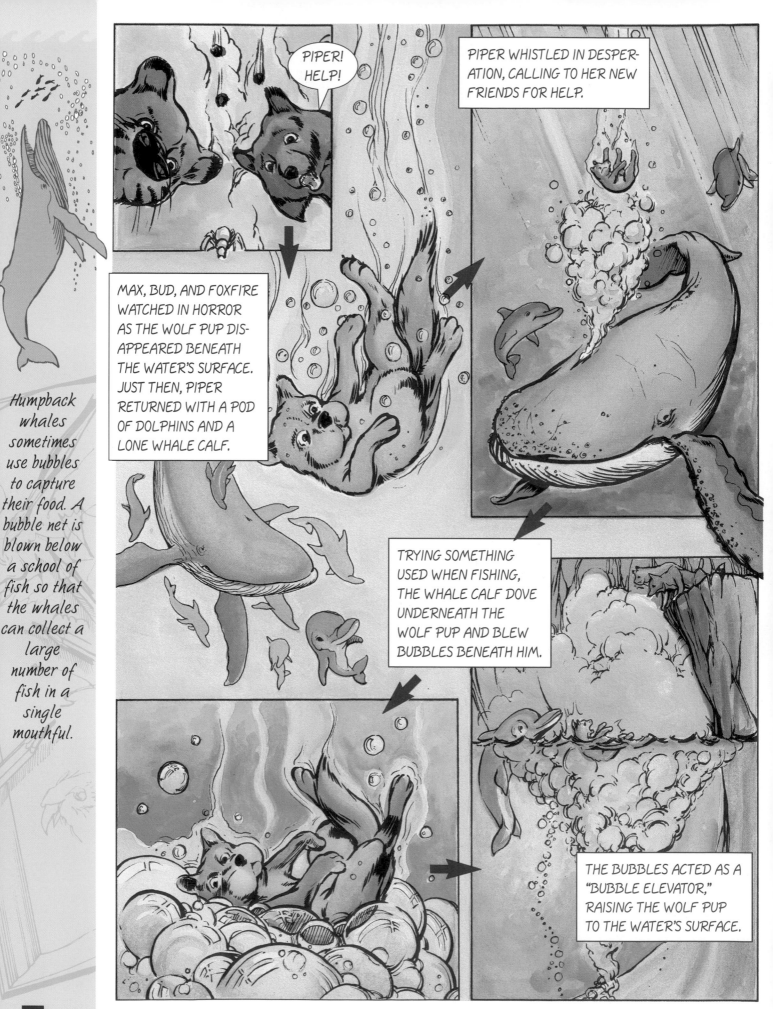

Humpback whales sometimes use bubbles to capture their food. A bubble net is blown below a school of fish so that the whales can collect a large number of fish in a single mouthful.

The dolphin has long been a symbol of beauty and intelligence. For centuries, sailors have told stories of dolphins saving drowning men and protecting them from circling sharks.

Shark

Dolphin

THE UNDERWATER TUNNEL IS OUR ONLY CHANCE. MY DOLPHIN FRIENDS AND I WILL USE ECHOLOCATION TO FIND THE WAY.

HURRY! YOU CAN DO IT! TAKE A DEEP BREATH AND WE'LL DO THE REST.

AS THE DOLPHINS AND THEIR PASSENGERS MADE THEIR WAY THROUGH THE TUNNEL, THE WALLS OF THE CAVE TUMBLED DOWN AROUND THEM.

All mammals must breathe air to survive. Like human beings and wolves, dolphins must hold their breath whenever they are underwater.

Many animals live in families or social groups. Protection and help in finding and catching food are two examples of the benefits of living in a group.

People

Bees

Wolves

Ants

Lions

IT WAS HARDER FOR THE TERRATROOPERS TO LEAVE TERRATOPIA THIS TIME. WITH EACH VISIT, THEIR FRIENDSHIP GREW STRONGER AND THEY MISSED EACH OTHER WHEN THEY WERE APART. YET THEY KNEW THERE WAS MUCH TO DO AT HOME.

DURING HIGH TIDE, PIPER ROWED A SMALL BOAT TO THE DEEPEST PART OF THE COVE. AS SHE HAD HOPED, CURIOUS SPOUTER SWAM BEHIND TOWARD THE OPEN SEA.

I KNOW YOU HAVE TO GO, BUT I'LL NEVER FORGET YOU.

THEY'RE WAITING FOR YOU OUT THERE.

GOOD-BYE! HAVE A GOOD, SAFE TRIP!

GEYSERS OF WATER SHOT INTO THE AIR AS SPOUTER SWAM TO JOIN THE REST OF THE POD.

THE END.

When you find young, wild animals be sure not to touch or move them – the parents are probably nearby, waiting for you to leave!

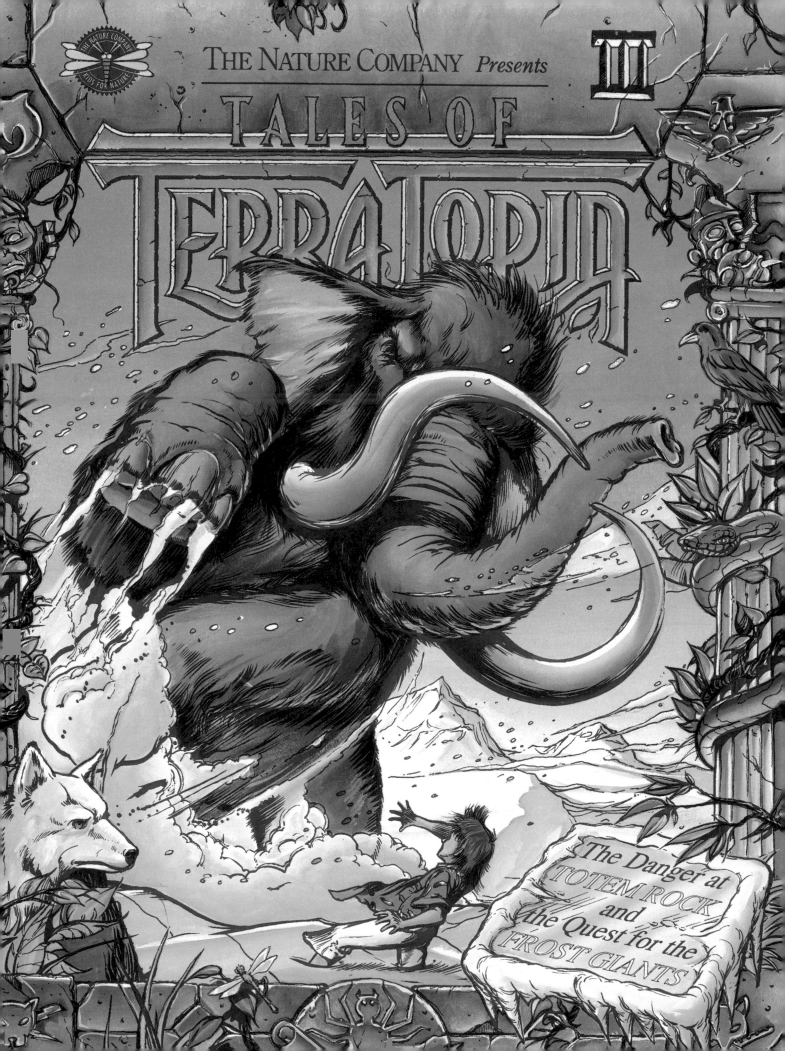

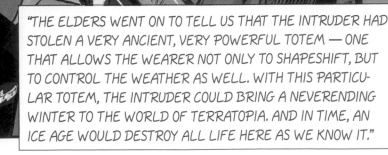

"IT WAS ALMOST TOO MUCH TO BELIEVE. WE WON-DERED IF THERE WERE ANY CLUES BURIED IN THE DISASTER THE INTRUDER HAD LEFT BEHIND. IT WOULD TAKE A WHILE TO FIGURE OUT WHAT, IF ANY-THING, WAS MISSING, BUT IT SEEMED WORTH A TRY."

"PIPER FOUND A SCRAP OF PAPER WITH A MESSAGE IN CODE BUT THAT WAS PRETTY MUCH IT."

"THINGS WERE GETTING KIND OF DESPERATE UNTIL THE ELDERS CAME UP WITH ONE MORE IDEA..."

THE ONLY HELP WE CAN OFFER IS THIS ANCIENT BOOK, "THE BOOK OF THE WHETHERBEEN."

"THE BOOK OF THE WHETHERBEEN" RECALLS THE STORIES OF ANIMALS THAT WE DON'T KNOW WHETHER OR NOT THEY'VE BEEN. THESE ANIMALS ARE STUFF OF LEGENDS LIKE THE PHOENIX, THE GRYPHON, AND THE UNICORN. ALSO, IN THIS BOOK, ARE THE ONLY KNOWN RECORDED MAPS OF TERRATOPIA'S UNCHARTED REGIONS TO THE NORTH. WHETHER THEY'RE ACCURATE, WE'RE NOT SURE.

"THE BOOK OF THE WHETHERBEEN" HAS BEEN PASSED DOWN THROUGH THE GENERATIONS. IT IS OUR ONLY SOURCE OF CLUES TO TERRATOPIA'S MYSTERIES. READ THE BOOK CAREFULLY, IT MAY REVEAL IMPORTANT CLUES THAT WILL AID YOU IN YOUR JOURNEY.

If found, please return to Sketch c/o Totem Rock, TerraTopia

"THE DAY WE OPENED 'THE BOOK OF THE WHETHERBEEN' WAS THE DAY I STARTED MY JOURNAL. IT WAS STARTING TO GET COMPLICATED AND I DIDN'T WANT TO FORGET ANYTHING THE ELDERS HAD SAID."

"WE POURED OVER THE PAGES OF THE BOOK SEARCHING FOR CLUES. WE FIGURED IF WE USED OUR WITS, WORKED AS A TEAM, AND THOUGHT LIKE SECRET AGENTS, WE COULD RESCUE BUD AND SAVE TERRATOPIA."

REMEMBER –
• we should think like secret agents
• Use our wits
• Trust our natural instincts
• Stay cool in the face of danger

"BEFORE WE HEADED NORTH, FOXFIRE THOUGHT WE SHOULD COMB THE HIDE-OUT FOR CLUES. PIPER SUGGESTED WE MIGHT LEARN EVEN MORE IF WE CHANGED INTO OUR ANIMAL TOTEMS."

"THE SPOOKY THING WAS, WE ALL FELT LIKE WE WERE BEING WATCHED — ALMOST FOLLOWED."

"FOXFIRE CHANGED INTO A FOX AND WITHIN MINUTES, USING HER NOSE AS HER GUIDE, SHE WAS HOT ON THE TRAIL OF THE INTRUDER... BUT STILL SHE WASN'T SURE."

"AS A SPIDER, MAX CHECKED OUT THOSE TINY PLACES THE REST OF US JUST COULDN'T GET TO. EVEN THERE, HE FELT THE INTRUDER'S PRESENCE."

TOP SECRET
ECO - AGENT TIPS

"SHADOW TRICKS

A Saber-Toothed Tiger

A Woolly Mammoth

An Alligator

INSTRUCTIONS FOR INVISIBLE INK

● NOTE: For absolute secrecy, write a message in Terra Topia's secret code language.

Step 1: Secure some paper and one of the following "inks"
• lemon juice OR • white vinegar OR • milk

Step 2: Dip a small paint brush OR the quill of a feather into the "ink" and write a secret message. Be sure to let dry completely.

Step 3: Deliver the message.   Step 4: To read the message, hold the paper close (BUT NOT TOO CLOSE) to the flame of a candle. The message will magically appear.

THE SNOW AND ICE CAME SHOWERING DOWN ON THE TERRATROOPERS. THERE WAS NO WAY TO OUTRUN IT... THERE WAS NOWHERE TO GO.

JUST WHEN IT LOOKED LIKE THIS MIGHT BE IT, THE LEDGE THE TERRATROOPERS HAD BEEN STANDING ON SNAPPED OFF AND BEGAN SLIDING DOWN THE MOUNTAIN FACE LIKE A BOBSLED OUT OF CONTROL.

DOWN AND DOWN IT SHOT, SPEEDING INTO THE FORESTS BELOW.

HO-O-OLD ON, GUYS! SEEING HOW I CAN'T FIND THE BRAKES, THIS IS GOING TO BE ONE WILD RIDE!

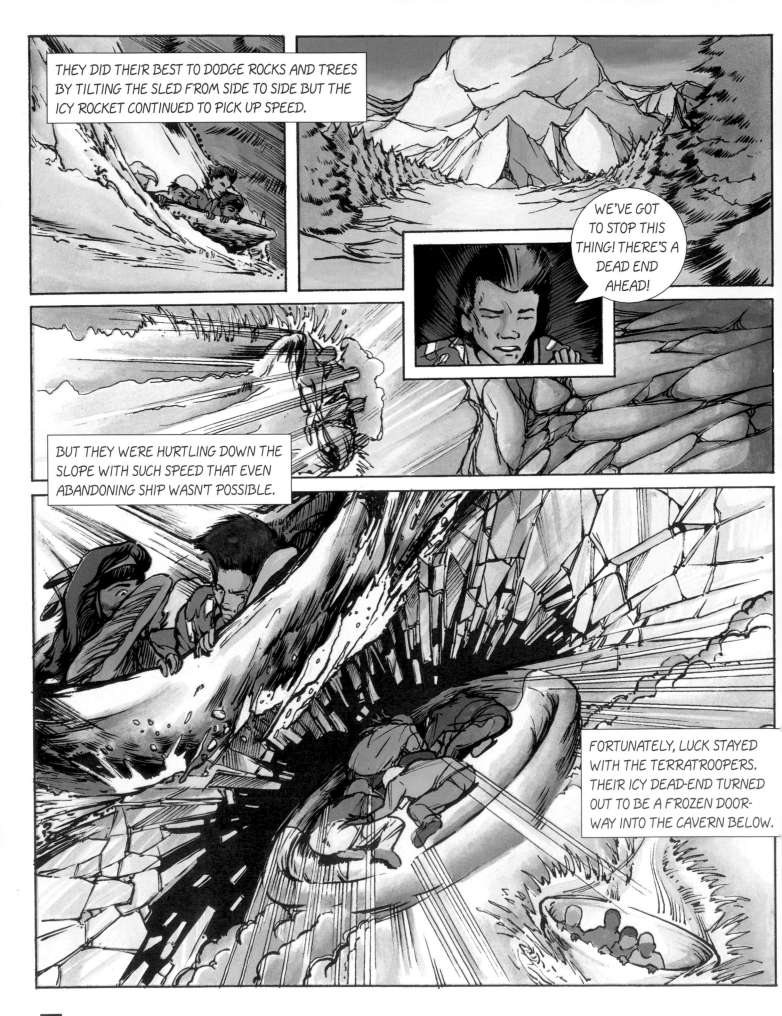

THEY DID THEIR BEST TO DODGE ROCKS AND TREES BY TILTING THE SLED FROM SIDE TO SIDE BUT THE ICY ROCKET CONTINUED TO PICK UP SPEED.

WE'VE GOT TO STOP THIS THING! THERE'S A DEAD END AHEAD!

BUT THEY WERE HURTLING DOWN THE SLOPE WITH SUCH SPEED THAT EVEN ABANDONING SHIP WASN'T POSSIBLE.

FORTUNATELY, LUCK STAYED WITH THE TERRATROOPERS. THEIR ICY DEAD-END TURNED OUT TO BE A FROZEN DOOR-WAY INTO THE CAVERN BELOW.

Hidden Animals

See if you can discover the five hidden animals:
Polar Bear
Saber-Toothed Tiger
Penguin
Walrus
Snowy Owl

Answers on page 117

Sketch

94

DON'T TELL ME... YOU MUST BE THE MYSTERIOUS FROST GIANTS. NO WONDER IT'S BEEN A SECRET. AND YOU'RE SUPPOSED TO HELP??

YIKES!

SKETCH WAS TORN BETWEEN BEING HAPPY THAT THEY'D FOUND THE FROST GIANTS OR BEING SCARED TO DEATH. HE WAS INCLINED TOWARD THE LATTER.

LIKE MAX ALWAYS SAYS, "I'VE GOT A BAD FEELING ABOUT THIS!"

TO BE CONTINUED...

BEASTLY BIOS

• Vegetarian

Tusks are 8-10 feet long.

Sometimes very old mammoths have crossed tusks.

Hump on back is made of fat. Fat is absorbed when there is no food.

13-14 feet in height at the shoulder.

Rust brown outer bristle-like coat of hair. Outer coat protects them from rain and snow.

Tusks are used for fighting and digging up roots to eat.

Soft, woolly, yellowish under fur for warmth.

Sketch

• Hunted by primitive man who trapped them in hidden pits in the ground.

• Last Earth Sighting: 11,000 years ago.

Clues from the Past:

"Ancient Carving"

"Cave Drawing"

THE TERRATROOPERS HAD MADE THE LONG JOURNEY NORTH THROUGH TERRATOPIA. THEY HAD SURVIVED A BLIZZARD; AN AVALANCHE; A DEATH-DEFYING RIDE ON AN OUT-OF-CONTROL ICE SLED DOWN A WALL OF SNOW; AND ICICLES AS SHARP AS RAZOR BLADES — ALL IN A DESPERATE ATTEMPT TO RESCUE BUD AND RECOVER THE STOLEN TOTEM THAT WAS SO POWERFUL, IN THE WRONG HANDS, IT COULD SEND TERRATOPIA INTO ANOTHER ICE AGE.
HEY, YOU GUYS! GET UP! I THINK WE FOUND 'EM!
WHY DIDN'T I THINK OF IT BEFORE!? WHAT ELSE COULD THE FROST GIANTS BE BUT WOOLLY MAMMOTHS?
I DON'T KNOW, BUT I WAS KIND OF HOPIN' THEY MIGHT BE MINUS THESE NASTY LOOKING TUSKS.

THE TERRATROOPERS' RELIEF AT HAVING DISCOVERED THE FROST GIANTS WAS SHORT-LIVED AS THE HERD PRESSED IN OMINOUSLY AROUND THEM. EVIDENTLY, THE WOOLLY MAMMOTHS BELIEVED THAT THEIR SECRET SANCTUARY WAS BEING THREATENED.
I THOUGHT THE FROST GIANTS WERE SUPPOSED TO HELP US.
YEAH. I'M NOT SURE WHAT THE ELDERS HAD IN MIND, BUT I'VE GOT A BAD FEELING ABOUT THIS.
SOMEHOW I DON'T THINK OUR TOTEMS ARE GOING TO DO US A WHOLE LOT OF GOOD.
WATCH OUT FOR THESE!
Animal responses to danger.
Snakes — Rattle or coil
Cats — Hiss
Owls — Screech
Wolves — Growl
Porcupine — Throw quills
Skunks — Squirt (P.U.!)
Herds — Stampede
Opossums — Play dead
Trilophodon 26-2 million years ago
Wooly Mammoth 2 million years ago
African Elephant Modern day
Reminds me of an elephant

WAIT! MAYBE THEY'LL RECOGNIZE "THE BOOK OF THE WHETHERBEEN."

...JUST ONE MORE INCH.

I'VE GOT IT!

SKETCH RAISED THE BOOK HIGH ABOVE HIS HEAD. AT THE SIGHT OF "THE BOOK OF THE WHETHERBEEN," THE WOOLLY MAMMOTHS DREW BACK IN SURPRISE.

LOOK, I THINK THEY RECOGNIZE THE BOOK.

SURE LOOKS THAT WAY.

DO YOU THINK THEY KNOW IT'S FROM THE ELDERS?

AT THAT MOMENT, A BABY FROST GIANT SQUEEZED ITS WAY BETWEEN THE TERRA-TROOPERS, SIGNALING THEIR ACCEPTANCE INTO THE HERD. FINALLY, IT LOOKED AS THOUGH THE TERRATROOPERS WERE GETTING SOMEWHERE.

MAYBE. THE FROST GIANTS SEEM A BIT FRIENDLIER NOW.

ROAR

SUDDENLY, A DEAFENING ROAR SHATTERED THE PEACEFUL GATHERING.

WATCH OUT! THE INTRUDER!

A VICIOUS-LOOKING SABER-TOOTHED TIGER PREPARED TO ATTACK ITS PREY. IN RESPONSE, THE WOOLLY MAMMOTHS FORMED A DEFENSIVE RING TO WARD OFF THE IMPENDING ATTACK. BUT THE BABY, NOT KNOWING ANY BETTER, TOOK OFF TOWARD THE MOUTH OF THE ICE CAVERN FROM WHICH THE TERRATROOPERS HAD JUST COME. SEEING AN EASY TARGET, THE SABER-TOOTH FOLLOWED IN HOT PURSUIT.

QUICK! WE'VE GOT TO SAVE THE CALF! AND WE'RE NOT GOING TO GET A WHOLE LOT OF HELP — THE REST OF THE WOOLLY MAMMOTHS WILL NEVER FIT THROUGH THAT ENTRANCE.

AS THE SABER-TOOTH SLOWLY MOVED IN TOWARD ITS PREY, THE LITTLE WOOLLY MAMMOTH CALF REACTED INSTINCTIVELY AND STRUCK A DEFENSIVE POSTURE, SHIELDING THE KIDS FROM DANGER.

SKETCH'S RIGHT. THINK ABOUT IT... THREE KIDS AND A BABY WOOLLY AREN'T MUCH OF A MATCH FOR HIS SET OF PRIMORDIAL CLAWS. BUT WHAT ABOUT A SURE-FOOTED FOX, AN AERIAL SET OF EAGLE CLAWS AND A HARD-TO-FIND INSECT? WE MIGHT JUST BE ABLE TO GIVE PIPER ENOUGH TIME TO GET OUR FRIEND OUT OF HERE.

MAYBE WE CAN HELP TOO.

THE BEST DEFENSE IS A GOOD OFFENSE... SO, TOTEMS ATTACK!

THE SABER-TOOTH CLEARLY WASN'T PREPARED FOR THIS SHOW OF COLLECTIVE COURAGE.

SKETCH, IN HIS EAGLE FORM, TOOK TO THE AIR, DIVE-BOMBING THE SABER-TOOTH WITH SWEEPS OF HIS CLAWS.

FOXFIRE, AS A FOX, TANGLED UP THE SURPRISED SABER-TOOTH'S FEET BY DODGING IN AND OUT OF ITS LEGS.

Fight or flight - what animals do in times of danger
Let's do both!

HEY YOU BIG OL' CAT! OVER HERE!

FOR HIS PART, MAX TAUNTED THE SABER-TOOTHED TIGER BY BEING IN ONE PLACE, THEN TURNING INTO A SPIDER, DISAPPEARING, AND THEN TURNING UP AGAIN IN THE FORM OF MAX SOMEWHERE ELSE.

FOR A MOMENT, IT LOOKED LIKE THE TERRATROOPERS WOULD WIN.

107

AS THE BATTLE WAGED ON, THE SABER-TOOTH GAINED THE HIGH GROUND. WITH ONE OF ITS HUGE PAWS, THE GIANT CAT PINNED FOXFIRE'S FOXTAIL TO THE SNOW.

THEN IT TACKLED MAX BEFORE HE WAS ABLE TO TRANSFORM INTO A SPIDER, AND TOSSED HIM INTO A SNOWY BANK WITH ONE SWIFT MOTION.

AT LAST, THE SNOW-ENCRUSTED CRUSADERS FOUND THEMSELVES FACE TO FACE WITH THE PREHISTORIC PREDATOR. FOXFIRE, SKETCH AND MAX FIGURED THEIR TIME WAS <u>REALLY</u> UP AS THE SABER-TOOTHED TIGER BARRED ITS FANGS AND BEGAN TO...

SKETCH MADE A FINAL VALIANT PASS AT THE GIANT CAT BUT WAS UNPREPARED FOR THE SABER-TOOTH'S LIGHTNING-SPEED LUNGE TO THE LEFT. UNABLE TO COMPENSATE, SKETCH SWERVED TO AVOID THE AWAITING CLAWS AND ENDED UP IN THE SNOW.

THE WOLF ELDER BEGAN: "BUD HAS COMPLETED HIS APPRENTICESHIP IN TERRA TOPIA. HE IS NOW READY TO APPLY HIS KNOWLEDGE AND WISDOM TO THE CHALLENGES OF HIS NATIVE FLORIDA. BUT BEFORE WE COULD LET HIM CONTINUE ON, WE HAD TO BE CERTAIN THAT THE REST OF YOU COULD MANAGE WITHOUT HIS HELP."

THE SNAKE ELDER CONTINUED: "BUD THOUGHT UP THE INTRUDER SCHEME AND INVENTED THE POWERFUL STOLEN TOTEM THAT WOULD LEAD YOU TO THE HIDDEN VALLEY OF THE FROST GIANTS. YOU WERE CLEVER AND RESOURCEFUL, USING YOUR WITS, SHAPESHIFTING POWERS, AND 'THE BOOK OF THE WHETHERBEEN,' TO MAKE A TRULY DIFFICULT JOURNEY. YOU CONFRONTED THE DANGERS WITH COURAGE AND EVEN PLACED YOUR OWN LIVES IN DANGER TO PROTECT THE YOUNG WOOLLY MAMMOTH. BUD SAID YOU COULD DO ALL OF THESE THINGS AND HE WAS RIGHT. WE ARE ALL VERY PROUD OF YOU AS YOU SHOULD BE OF YOURSELVES."

GOOD-BYES WERE NEVER EASY AND THIS PARTICULAR GOOD-BYE WAS THE HARDEST OF ALL. BUD HAD EXCITING ADVENTURES AHEAD OF A DIFFERENT KIND, BUT HE WOULD NEVER FORGET TERRATOPIA OR THE TERRATROOPERS. HE LEFT PIPER, MAX, SKETCH, AND FOXFIRE WITH ONE FINAL WORD OF ADVICE.

I THINK THE BIGGEST LESSON I LEARNED IS THAT AS ONE OF THE TERRATROOPERS, YOU MUST ALWAYS USE YOUR MIND TO RESCUE NATURE PROPERLY. IF YOU DON'T, YOU CAN BECOME JUST AS BIG A PROBLEM AS THE ONE YOU'RE TRYING TO SOLVE.

I'LL MISS YOU GUYS BUT REMEMBER, I'LL ONLY BE A RAVEN'S CALL AWAY.

AND WITH THAT, THE FIRST YEAR OF ADVENTURES OF THE TERRATROOPERS DREW TO A CLOSE.

THE END

Dear Friend:

You know from reading our first adventure in TerraTopia that the Elders introduced us to our animal totems when we were high up on the cliffs of Totem Rock. They told us that everyone has an animal totem, including you. Your totem is an animal you will learn to listen to. Each totem is the representation of yourself, a mirrored spirit of who you are, or would be, in the natural world.

MAX's totem is SPIDER. Spider is really good at making connections between things. Spider weaves plans and spins ideas much like it weaves a web.

PIPER has chosen DOLPHIN. Dolphin loves the water and its "laughter" seems to echo across the waves. Piper and Dolphin share a playful spirit and a love of life.

SKETCH's special animal is EAGLE. Eagle has excellent eyesight and perception. We always admire the way Sketch sees patterns in nature and uncovers the tiny signs left by quiet visitors that the rest of us might miss without him.

FOXFIRE was named for FOX. Fox is swift and intelligent. By understanding its surroundings and becoming a part of them, Fox can outwit almost any challenger. Foxfire has this same incredible ability. She's a great person to have on your team.

Finally, it's no surprise that BUD's totem is MOUNTAIN LION. Both of them are strong, powerful, and can outrun us all. Mountain Lion is a graceful, courageous leader who promotes teamwork and problem solving.

In addition to our animal totems, we've selected special stones that symbolize qualities we'd each like to have, or they remind of us of words of wisdom when things get a little dicey.

Since you're one of the TerraTroopers too, we figured it was important for you to choose an animal totem, special stone, codename, and your very own way of coming To the Rescue. We're giving you a few ideas (some we got from the Elders) but don't feel limited by what we've written here. You can make whatever choices work for you.

Have fun!
Your friends,

Piper   Bud   Foxfire   MAX
                              Sketch

Join the TerraTroopers

Totally Totem

ALLIGATOR

is one of the largest living members of the reptile family. Alligator is protected by its scales that form a natural coat of armor. Alligator can be a dangerous enemy as easily as a powerful friend.

DEER

dwells in the peacefulness of the forest. Although Deer shows great speed and agility as it leaps through the air, Deer is generally a gentle, graceful creature with the power to touch the hearts of others.

FROG

is a solitary creature who can live almost anywhere. Frog's croaking chorus is often heard rising from the pond in which it lives. Frog's song speaks to us of metamorphosis as it changes from a tadpole swimming in murky waters to its mature adult state when Frog is at home both on land or in water.

BEAR

understands and revels in the changes of the season. During the cold winter months, Bear finds peace in the silence of hibernation. And in the springtime, Bear re-emerges from its sleep ready to enjoy and embrace the world. What Bear lacks in speed, it makes up for in power. Its strong claws can swipe through the air with great force. But Bear often balances its ferocious side by searching for honey, showing its preference for the sweetness of life.

DRAGONFLY

has iridescent wings that remind us of the special and unique things in life. Dragonfly has keen eyesight thanks to its compound lenses — sometimes up to 30,000 lenses. In some cultures, Dragonfly is believed to foretell changes of events to come. Regardless, Dragonfly can use its powerful vision to look past the obvious and focus on the underlying truth.

GIRAFFE

is the world's tallest animal. Its height is its defense, for Giraffe's long neck allows it to observe its enemies before itself being observed. Giraffe moves slowly and with grace through the boughs of the trees. Giraffe also suggests resilience given its ability to go for long periods of time without water and requiring little sleep.

BUTTERFLY

is a beautiful four-winged creature whose delicate patterns are made up of tiny scales. Butterfly symbolizes transformation and the opportunity to change, making dreams become a reality as they take flight. Butterfly has a highly developed sense of smell and feeds on the sweetness of nectar.

ELEPHANT

is the largest living land animal and is both intelligent as well as majestic in stature. Elephant's unique trunk gives it great versatility. The trunk allows Elephant to carry food and water to its mouth, spray water, smell, investigate, and lift objects. Elephant can also sleep either standing up or lying down.

HORSE (WILD)

runs with the wind at its hooves — flying through the open grasslands. Throughout history, Horse has represented grace and sensitivity as well as swiftness.

KOALA

is an expert climber who moves with great agility from tree to tree avoiding the ground whenever possible. It is a highly selective creature who carefully avoids unnecessary exposure to the outside world. Koala's protective nature aids it in caring for its young who are carried in its pouch.

MOUSE

is adaptable and resourceful, making it a small but important member of any team. Mouse knows through experience how to use its size to its advantage as it moves in and out of spaces forbidden to other animals. Mouse is very sensitive to details and saves tiny treasures for future use.

OWL

is a bird of prey shrouded by the mystery of the night. It flies almost without a sound and attacks its prey without warning. Owl has excellent eyesight and an acute sense of hearing. The placement of Owl's eyes on its flat face gives it binocular vision. Owl symbolizes wisdom. Its powerful senses allow it to know things that others cannot.

SEA OTTER

is sleek and playful, always making the most of life. As an expert swimmer and noted acrobat, Sea Otter combines the excitement of exploration with the simple joys of curiosity and discovery. Sea Otter is also very resourceful, using tools such as stones to smash open shells.

SHARK

is a creature of ancient mystery. Its history extends back more than 500 million years. A feared hunter through the ages, Shark's strengths are its sharp teeth, sense of smell, and its speed. But Shark must also swim constantly to avoid sinking.

SNAKE

feels and knows the power of nature. It is able to shed its skin and be reborn each year and so accumulates the wisdom that comes from all creation. Snake does not wish to intrude upon the world of others, but if threatened, will respond with quick, decisive action. Snake is a reminder of the ancient world — a link to a time when reptiles ruled the Earth. Those whose animal totem is snake are rare indeed.

SQUIRREL

plans ahead and is always prepared. Squirrel can also circle branches at lightning speed. Because Squirrel is quick and anticipates what lies ahead, it can effectively meet the challenges it confronts.

WOLF

is the teacher with keen eyes and ears who shares its knowledge and insight with its family — the family of all living things. The lead wolf often stands alone, out in front, trying to show the rest of the pack the way to understanding all of the great mysteries of life.

WHALE

understands and embraces change. It has evolved over 60-70 million years from a land mammal. What were once front limbs are now powerful flippers. In spite of its size, Whale is most often gentle and has a powerful ability to listen and interpret communications.

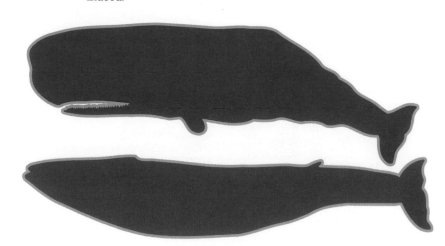

Rock 'n' Roll

AMETHYST (*Foxfire's stone*) is a beautiful purple crystalline quartz usually found in volcanic rock. Amethyst is a symbol of spiritual power. Amethyst represents intuitive awareness and sensitivity to the world.

AGATE (*Bud's stone*) is a sign of strength, security and balance. Agate represents support and protection of others and is believed to bring good luck to those who wear it. The agate is a mineral formed slowly over time by pressure and slow cooling of the rocks around it.

AVENTURINE (*Max's stone*) is a sign of motivation and opportunity. Ancient people decorated the eyes of their statues with aventurine to symbolically increase visionary powers. Aventurine is a quartz tightly packed full of chrome-rich mica crystals.

FOSSIL signifies timelessness and reminds us that we should draw strength and understanding from lessons learned in the past.

GARNET is a stone of the soul, usually found in shades of red. It promotes self-esteem and stimulates the imagination. Garnet comes from the Latin word, "granatus," meaning "like pomegranate seeds" and that's just what they look like: "seeds within other rocks".

JADE is a symbol of peace and serenity. It encourages you to think about what is good, not bad, about any given situation. Look to the stone as a symbol of justice, wisdom and balance.

JASPER helps you think on your feet. Jasper is said to teach us patience and perseverance even when the going gets tough. Its opaque hardness is like that of an agate and it comes in many shades from red, brown, and yellow, to green.

MALACHITE is a soft, sensitive stone that offers us power through self-understanding. Its beautiful deep green color, often highlighted with bands of lighter green, comes from copper.

PERIDOT is a transparent olive green (or sometimes yellow) stone composed of magnesium iron silicate. Look to this stone for the courage, confidence, and patience required of a wise leader.

ROSE QUARTZ (*Piper's stone*) is one of the most valued types of quartz crystals because it rarely actually forms crystals. It possesses both beauty and strength and represents friendship and a love of life.

TIGER'S EYE (*Sketch's stone*) supports an insightful perception of the world. Those who possess the Tiger's Eye are clear of thought and keen of vision. A form of quartz, Tiger's Eye has bands of yellow and brown formed by fibers of the mineral crocidolite. Each of the lines in the stone represents the narrow iris of an eagle's or cat's eye. Tiger's Eye encourages imagination and artistic inspiration.

TOURMALINE represents peace, harmony, wisdom and willpower. If you are able to discover a state of contentment within yourself, you will also unleash your creative spirit. Tourmaline is from a family of aluminum silicate minerals mixed with various metals that is generally found as crystals in granite. It suggests harmony by often appearing in two different colors side by side, such as pink and green.

TURQUOISE is often reserved for visionary people. It is for those who strive to fulfill their dreams in spite of the many challenges they may face along the path. Turquoise is a hydrous copper aluminum sulfate found in blues, greenish blues and deep greens.

Source: Stone Power, by Dorothee L. Mella, Warner Books, Inc., New York, NY 1986.

Pick a Rock! Here's some rocks to choose from or pick another favorite!

Choose a Codename

Try to think of one or two words that describe you and relate to the animal totem you've just chosen. To give you some ideas, we've included our codenames but remember that there are lots and lots of possibilities! After that, try writing your codename in the TerraTopia Secret Code Language — it's extra secret!

WAVE DANCER (Piper)

〰️ symbols

WILD SPIRIT (Foxfire)

〰️ symbols

FAST CAT (Bud)

〰️ symbols

SKY RIDER (Sketch)

〰️ symbols

SPINNER (Max)

〰️ symbols

Come to the Rescue

The last step to becoming an official member of the TerraTroopers is figuring out your own special way to come TO THE RESCUE.

Here are our personal favorites:

If you recycle your family's newspaper every day for a year, you will save 4 trees. Since a tree has to be at least 25 years old to be cut for paper, by recycling newspapers you save 100 years of tree life.

Sketch

I try to keep my ocean friends safe by using as little plastic as possible. Each year 1,000,000 (1 million) sea birds and 100,000 ocean mammals (like dolphins and whales) die from eating plastic or getting tangled up in it. If you buy sodas in 6 packs, cut the plastic rings into small pieces so the animals won't get caught.

Piper

The Elders have told me to step lightly in nature so I try to treat all living things with respect. "Leave only your footprints and take away only your memories."

Foxfire

My vote is for recycling aluminum cans. I heard that 92 billion aluminum cans are used every year in the U.S. alone. If we could line up those cans end to end, they would go from the earth to the moon and back about 30 and one half times. That's way too many round trips if you ask me. Let's just reuse the cans we've got!

MAX

Yo! I ride my bike whenever I can. Using gasoline produces gases that pollute the air and don't let the heat from the sun out of the atmosphere. It's called "global warming" and some call it the "greenhouse effect." So I keep my legs pumping and the wheels turning!

Bud

Answer Page

PAGE 46 Constellations

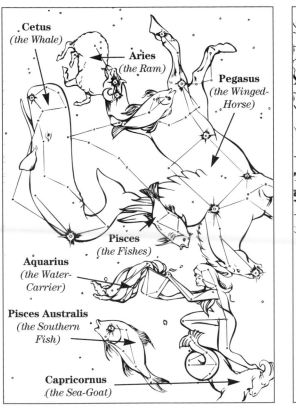

Cetus
(the Whale)

Aries
(the Ram)

Pegasus
(the Winged-
Horse)

Pisces
(the Fishes)

Aquarius
(the Water-
Carrier)

Pisces Australis
(the Southern
Fish)

Capricornus
(the Sea-Goat)

PAGE 54 Hidden Animals

Hidden Animals

See if you can discover the seven hidden animals:
caribou
wolf
goose
dragonfly
squirrel
monarch butterfly
raven

Sketch

PAGE 55

A mouse is traveling along. A deer arrives. A mountain lion ignores the mouse and chases the deer. The mouse continues its journey. An eagle spots the mouse's movement with its excellent eyesight and swoops down for dinner. The eagle continues its journey.

PAGE 63 Migration Patterns

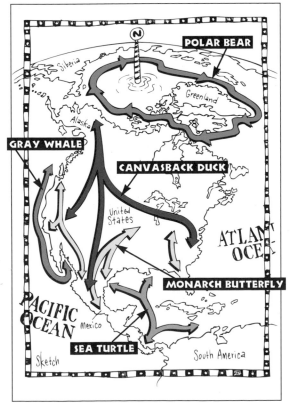

N

POLAR BEAR

Siberia

Greenland

Alaska

GRAY WHALE

CANVASBACK DUCK

United States

ATLAN
OCE

MONARCH BUTTERFLY

PACIFIC OCEAN

Mexico

SEA TURTLE

South America

Sketch

PAGE 94 Hidden Animals

Hidden Animals

See if you can discover the five hidden animals:
Polar Bear
Saber-Toothed Tiger
Penguin
Walrus
Snowy Owl

ANSWER TO JOKE ON PAGE 64

Kids 4 Nature, better known as "K4N" is "Nature with an Attitude." It communicates the idea that "We matter and we have something to give to the world" through innovative, high-quality, product-based experiences. Because K4N is first and foremost directed toward kids, the products and overall program speak to kids in their language, through their images and with respect to their sensibilities about the importance of nature and their role in the world at large.

TerraTopia Concept: Karla "Wild Horse" Kelly, Vicki "Gazelle" Dobbs, Steve "Peregrine Falcon" Beck

Tales by: Steve "Peregrine Falcon" Beck, Karla "Wild Horse" Kelly, Vicki "Gazelle" Dobbs

Penciller: Steve "Peregrine Falcon" Beck

Inkers: Steve "Peregrine Falcon" Beck (Tales II, III, IV), Tim Burgard (Tale I)

Colorists: Gloria "Koala Bear" Vasquez, Sam "Wolf" Parsons

Graphic Designer: Mark "Raccoon" Shepard

"Sketch's Sketch Pad": Peter "Sea Otter" Chan, Charlie Ramos

The Graphic Adventure Cover Art: David McMacken with contributions from Jim Nichols, Steve "Peregrine Falcon" Beck

Individual Tales Cover Art: Steve "Peregrine Falcon" Beck (Tales II, III, IV); David McMacken (Tale I)

Educational Designer: Karla "Wild Horse" Kelly

Editor: Vicki "Gazelle" Dobbs

Contributing Editors: Harriet "Vespers Bat" Crosby, Jill "Mink" Jurkowitz, Adrienne "Fiddler Crab" Biggs

Special thanks to Roger Bergen, Carolyn Knutson, Sparrow Hawk, Steve Manning, The Meltons, Peter Revers and Priscilla Wrubel for making the magic of TerraTopia come alive.

TerraTopia: The Graphic Adventure, The First Four Tales
published by The Nature Company, Berkeley, CA, 94710.

Tales of TerraTopia: The Secret of the Dragonfly & The Daring Dino Rescue, and *Tales of TerraTopia: The Wandering Wolves in Vulcan's Vent*, first published in 1993.

Kids 4 Nature, K4N, Tales of TerraTopia, TerraTopia are trademarks of The Nature Company.

The stories, characters, and incidents featured in this book are entirely fictional.

Printed in the U.S.A. on recycled paper.
ISBN 1-883871-02-6